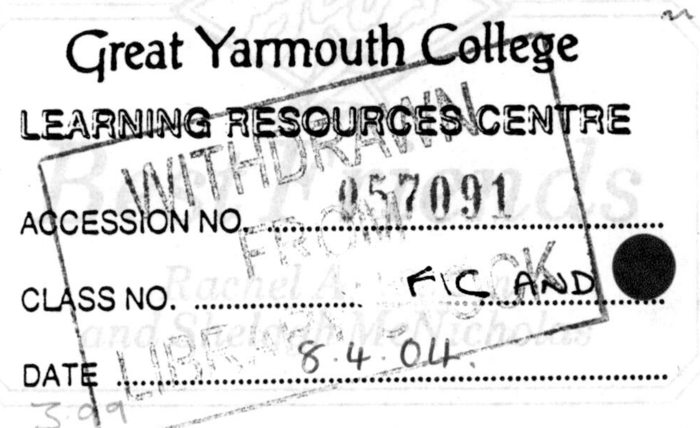

Look out for more *Jets* from Collins

Jessy Runs Away • **Rachel Anderson**
Ivana the Inventor • *Ernest the Heroic Lion Tamer* • **Damon Burnard**
Two Hoots • *Almost Goodbye Guzzler* • **Helen Cresswell**
Shadows on the Barn • **Sara Garland**
Nora Bone • *The Mystery of Lydia Dustbin's Diamonds* • **Brough Girling**
Thing on Two Legs • *Thing in a Box* • **Diana Hendry**
Desperate for a Dog • *More Dog Trouble* • *Rose Impey*
Georgie and the Dragon • *Georgie and the Planet Raider* • **Julia Jarman**
Free With Every Pack • **Robin Kingsland**
Mossop's Last Chance • *Mum's the Word* • **Michael Morpurgo**
Hiccup Harry • *Harry Moves House* • **Chris Powling**
Rattle and Hum, Robot Detectives • **Frank Rodgers**
Our Toilet's Haunted • **John Talbot**
Rhyming Russell • *Messages* • *Pat Thomson*
Monty the Dog Who Wears Glasses • *Monty's Ups and Downs* • **Colin West**
Ging Gang Goolie, it's an Alien • *Stone the Crows, it's a Vacuum Cleaner* • **Bob Wilson**

Published by A & C Black Ltd in 1991,
by Young Lions in 1992 and reprinted by Collins in 1995
15
Collins is an imprint of HarperCollins*Publishers* Ltd,
77-85 Fulham Palace Road, Hammersmith, London W6 8JB

The HarperCollins website address is
www.fireandwater.com

ISBN 0 00 674138 X

A CIP record for this title is available from the British Library.

Printed in Great Britain by
Clays Ltd, St Ives plc

When Jessy got home from school

her mum was there to meet her at the gate. So was Waffle, wagging his tail.

But her sister wasn't there.

Jessy wondered where she was.

But Jessy wasn't always very good at remembering things.

She wondered how long her sister would be away.

So Jessy and her mum had tea together.

It was quiet without Anna there. Jessy wished she'd come back.

The following Wednesday when Jessy got off the bus, Anna was already home from school as usual. There was another girl there too.

Jessy didn't know who she was.

'Ah, best friend from school,' said Jessy.

Jessy didn't go to the same school as her sister. She went to a special one where the teachers knew about helping people with learning difficulties.

'At *our* school,' said Anna's friend, Becky, 'Anna sits next to me, don't you Anna?'
Anna nodded.

'And she plays with me at playtime too.'

At *her* school, Jessy had to sit next to a boy called Mark. They didn't ever play together.

Anna's friend ran outside to play,
and Anna went after her.

Jessy felt lonely.
She wished *she* had
a best friend.

'No friend,'
she told
her mum.

Of course you've got friends,'
said her mother. 'Lots of them.
Your teacher. And all those nice
children at school.'
Jessy didn't think Mark was nice.
He liked kicking.

'Well, there's Dad,' her mum went on.
'And me.'

Jessy thought to herself, that's different. A mum was a mum. She said, 'You're my mum'.
'Can't I be your friend as *well* as your mum?' said Jessy's mum.

But Jessy wanted a friend, like Anna's friend, Becky – someone who was her own size and liked doing the same things.

At the sound of his name, Waffle looked up hopefully.

He thought it was time for a walk.

'And Snuffles is your friend too,' said Mum. 'Look, why not take him this nice piece of carrot?'

So Jessy wandered out
into the back garden
and looked at
her rabbit.

But Snuffles couldn't talk, and
Snuffles couldn't play and Snuffles
didn't ever laugh.

Even when Jessy pushed the carrot
through the wire netting,
all Snuffles did
was wriggle
his nose.

‘Snuffles,’ said Jessy. ‘No good.’
And she went in and stood by the window feeling sad.

Her mum knew she was miserable.

She fetched
her down some
jigsaws from
the top shelf.

But Jessy
didn't want
to do jigsaws.
She didn't
want to
watch television
either. She wanted
Anna's friend to go
away so she could
have Anna to herself.

While she was looking out of
the window, Jessy noticed
a big van, nearly as big as
a house, come slowly along
the street.
It stopped beside
the house next door.

Next door had been empty for
a long time.
Two people got out and began
lifting things from their van.
Jessy watched them

Chairs
and
tables.

Books
and boxes.

Pots and pans.

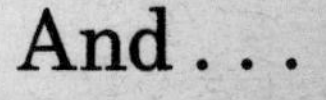

And . . .

a baby's
cot.

They put some of
the things down
in the next door
front garden,

and carried
some of them
into the next
door house,

and left
some of them
standing
around on
the pavement.
Jessy watched
what was going
on and soon
cheered up.
It's always
interesting
watching other
people busy
doing something.

Then Jessy's mum called everyone for tea.

Anna
and Becky
came
galumphing
down the stairs.

There was a special cake for tea, with chocolate topping.

Although Anna was younger than Jessy, Anna sometimes had to explain things to her.

Anna's friend giggled.

Jessy always tried not to mind when she heard people say bad things about her.

Jessy was glad that Anna always tried to stand up for her.

But after tea, Becky started again.

Jessy heard her whispering.

'Me too,' said Jessy.
She started to follow.
But Jessy
wasn't very
good at
doing things
fast.

Becky had already reached Anna's room and slammed the door shut before Jessy was even halfway up.

Jessy went down again slowly and sat on the swing under the apple tree doing nothing.

She wished it was time for Becky to go away. Then Anna and Jessy would be able to play together again.

Suddenly
Jessy heard
a noise
behind her.

She turned and saw a small boy
crawling through the hedge.

She wondered where he had
come from.

He began to tell her something, but Jessy couldn't understand what he was trying to say.

Then she saw that he was stuck. His jersey was caught on a branch. He couldn't go forwards and he couldn't go backwards.

She yelled loudly.

She knew someone
would come and help.

A woman's face looked through the hedge.

'Ah, so *that's* where he's got to!' said the woman.

'Got to?' said Jessy.

The woman from next door, with help from Jessy, managed to unhook the boy's jersey. Then she lifted him back over the hedge.

Jessy knew she was a lot more than three.

And whats your name?
Jessy.
That's a nice name.
D'you want to come over and play?

Jessy peered through the gap in the hedge that Tom had made. Tom's garden looked good.

He hadn't got a swing or a rabbit hutch. But the grass was tall and wild like a jungle and there was an interesting-looking shed that might be good for hiding in.

She really wanted to
go over. But then she
shook her head. She
knew that she mustn't
go off with people,
however nice they
seemed, unless
she'd asked her
mum first.
'Can't,' she said. 'No.'

Jessy smiled and said, 'Goodbye,'
then ran in to find her mum to tell
her about the boy next door.

But on the way she saw Anna and Becky coming down the stairs. Becky was giggling and Jessy heard her say,

But Becky went on saying it. 'She's got a silly face,' she sang and then she began to jump up and down chanting.

Silly!
Silly!
Silly hands!
Silly!
Silly! face!
Silly!
Silly!
Silly!

Jessy was very annoyed. She went into the kitchen and kicked her feet crossly against a chair.

'That girl!' she said. 'Still here!'

But her mum took no notice.

And Jessy ran into the hall.

Becky's school bag lay on the table. Jessy grabbed hold of it, held it upside down and shook it hard –

so that all Becky's things tumbled onto the floor in a muddle.

Then Jessy stamped on them.
And as she stamped, she

Anna came running.

Jessy stamped on the painting again. This time it tore.

Jessy's mum came to see what all
the commotion was about.
When she saw what Jessy had done
she was very
angry.

But Jessy didn't ever want to say sorry.

Even if Jessy's been upset, she can't get away with doing that sort of thing.

So then Becky
began to cry.

Soon Anna
was crying
too,

Waffle was
making sad
noises outside
the back door

and even
Mum looked
as though
she was going
to start
crying.

She carefully
picked up
Becky's things,

straightened
the painting,

gave Becky a hug,
and said, 'Sorry'.
Becky said
sorry too.

I think what everybody needs now is a good bit of nose blowing and a nice soothing drink.

She led them all into the kitchen.

Jessy could see it was Tom and he was stuck in the hedge again.
Stuck

And they ran out to help.

Tom looked rather worried until he recognised Jessy.
Then he smiled.

'He knows you already!' said Anna with surprise.

'My friend,' said Jessy. 'Tom lives next door.'

Tom's shoe had come off. He didn't seem to be able to get it on again.

Becky took it from him and tried to put it on for him.

But he didn't want her to help.
He wanted Jessy.

Tom's mum came looking for Tom.

'I'm afraid Tom's been a bit confused by the house-move,' Tom's mum explained. 'Being in a strange place, and having to leave all our old friends behind.'

So the following week when Becky came to tea again, Tom was invited over too.

They all played
together until
it was
tea-time.

Then they all sat round together on the grass,

Anna and her old best friend, Becky,

and Jessy and her new best friend Tom.

'It's good having friends to tea, isn't it?' said Anna.

Jessy thought it was and passed the pink cakes round again.